Story "A Tooth Fairy for Christmas"

2019 ©Copyright by Hiam Mondini

English version by Emily Ulbert

Proofreading by Nicholas Modlin

Book Cover drawing by Aurelio Romano Mondini

Print and Published by BoD – Books on Demand, Norderstedt

ISBN: 9783750424548

1

# "A Tooth Fairy for Christmas"

## Christmas Scene I

by

Hiam Mondini & Emily Ulbert

inspired in Chicago 2019

## Introduction

How many Christmas stories are there? A thousand? A hundred thousand? Millions? Probably more. Nevertheless, I will also write down a short Christmas story and immortalize it with an ISBN number. Why do I do this? Because I really like Christmas, the original Christmas Story still makes me cry, and I think there are not enough Christmas stories left to remind humanity why certain cultures actually celebrate this festival of love. With that spirit in mind, lots of love and coziness, care and attention.

Sunday

"Mommy!       Mommmyyy    !! Moooommmmmmmmyyyyy!!!!"

Bella screams through the small apartment as if her mother were standing on the other side of the city.

"What's going on?  Bella?  Are you all right, sweetheart?"  At lightning speed, Laurie runs into her daughter's bedroom and finds Bella sitting on the bed, her little fingers smeared with blood and a big grin on her face.  She triumphantly holds up something small in her hand.

"It's out!  My tooth is out!  Do you think the Tooth Fairy will come here tonight and pick it up?"  She happily lets her tongue dance over her teeth and explore the new space in her mouth.

"Oh, how great! You got it out.  Now I don't have to puree your apples anymore. You can bite again.  Let's see your trophy."

Although exhausted, Laurie goes to her daughter's bed and sits down beside Bella. She takes the blood-smeared tooth from the little girl's hand and admires it.

"Come on, let's wash the blood off. Then it will look even better. You gave me a nice scare there." Both rise from the knitted blanket Bella's grandmother made her and head to the small bathroom next door.

"Mom, do you think the Tooth Fairy will come tonight? Remember when Anne lost her tooth? The Tooth Fairy brought her a beautiful Barbie doll. And in the Barbie purse there was even some money." The little girl holds her curly-haired head to one side, her big saucer eyes sparkling at her sad mother.

"Oh, that was a very generous Tooth Fairy. She probably saw the big, beautiful house where she lives and thought a Barbie would belong in it." No sooner had Laurie finished her sentence, she regrets it and pinches her eyes together.

Before she can cover for her mistake, Bella is already speaking, "You mean, the Tooth Fairy brings different things to different houses?" Laurie bites her lower lip and looks carefully at her daughter. Then, she looks around worried. Wrinkling her forehead, her eyes rest on the tooth in her hand.

Bella continues to consult her mother, "I thought the Tooth Fairy would be really proud of me for giving her such a beautiful tooth. You know, Anne's tooth wasn't very good. It was all small because it stayed in her mouth so long."

Bella's eyes wander. She looks out the bathroom door directly into the living room, which serves her mother as a bedroom. As her gaze drifts away from the kitchen setup in the corner, she purses her lips, sighs and lifts her shoulders to shrug slightly. "Well, we'll see Mommy..."

"What do you think, Sweetie, if we don't put the tooth in front of the window today, but keep for a few more days to admire it?" The hopeful mother bends down to her daughter and grabs the tooth from her hand. Holding it between her fingers, she lifts it up to the light, rotating it as if it were a freshly cut diamond.

"That's a good idea, Mom. We can put it in front of the picture of Dad, then he can see it too. He would be proud of me, don't you think, Mommy?" Bella's excited eyes sparkle at her mother.

"Oh, I am very sure of that, Sweetie. Your Dad would be very proud of you and your monstrous tooth," she replies with a smile. Then she tickles her daughter's stomach, just like Adam used to.

Bella goes to the dining table and puts her cleaned tooth directly in front of a framed photograph of a smiling man. "Look, Daddy, my first tooth is out. Take good care of it; soon I will give it to the Tooth Fairy. We're curious what she'll give me in return. Sleep well, I love you." She kisses her small palm and then gently lays it on the glass.

Her mother quickly wipes away a tear and takes her daughter by the hand. "Well, then off to bed with you. Tomorrow starts the last week before Christmas break, and I'm pretty sure you have a lot of great things going on in Kindergarten." Laurie covers her little one with the knitted blanket, gives her a good night kiss and turns off the small light next to the bed. "Sweet dreams. See you tomorrow."

As she walks out of the room, she hears the sleepy words of her beloved little girl, "You too mommy and don't worry ..."

Monday

"No, Ma, I still can't get a widow's pension because we weren't married." Laurie closes her eyes, rubs the cold fingers of her free hand over them, then rests her hand on her hip. Pressing the phone in her other hand to her ear while she now looks at the sidewalk in front of her.

"I know Ma. I know. But I can't change that now... I just wanted to let you know that, unfortunately, we won't be able to fly home for Christmas. You understand, don't you?"

Feeling lost she looks around, as if she is hoping to get a little bit of understanding from somewhere. For a moment, she catches the eye of a man who is waiting to cross the street.

"But Ma, how am I supposed to do that? The rent, the insurance, taxes, Christmas presents, and now even the

Tooth Fairy! It's not my fault that the bookshop closed and I have to look for a new job now. They aren't throwing part-time jobs at single mothers. I just went to the employment agency. It would be really helpful now if you at least ... No, I don't want any money, you know that Mom."

Frustratedly, she throws her now very cold hand into the air. Blowing out a cloud of breath into the cold, she returns the phone to her ear as she enters the crosswalk.

"It's good, Mom. It's all right! I know you mean well, but I have to go through this myself. I know, for me it's not the same ... I don't know yet ... I'm going to the House of Hope tomorrow. I'll find something there for Bella. Maybe we'll celebrate Christmas with Mary. As soon as I can, we'll come and visit you. Promise. Give Daddy a kiss for me and we'll call on Christmas. Bye Mom."

She finishes the phone call with a deep sigh, puts the phone away and keeps her hand in the warmth of her jacket pocket.

Tuesday

"I'm sorry, no Barbies have come in recently. Maybe you'll be luckier next week. You never know what people want to get rid of before Christmas. Does it necessarily have to be a Barbie? We have lots of dolls in the toy corner." The old woman, behind the sales counter in the House of Hope, points with her crooked finger in the direction of the toy corner.

"No, it doesn't have to, but that would have been the first choice for the Tooth Fairy to bring. I'll have a look around again, thanks for checking." Laurie gives the volunteer a final smile and heads for the toy corner. Her gaze sweeps thoughtfully through the shelves and lands on something on an upper shelf that catches her attention. She leans her head to the side and wrinkles her forehead as she approaches for a closer look.

As soon as she makes it to the shelf, about to stretch out her hand, she is jostled from the side and a girl screams, "Maaaaammmaaaa! I want that!" Small, fleshy hands try to reach for it, but Laurie is faster. Using both hands, she quickly grabs the snowy glass ball and brings it in to her chest.

"Nooooo! That belongs to me! I saw it first! Maaaaammmaaaa, the evil lady took my ball! "

The small, pudgy face turns red and all the people in the resale shop seem to be holding their breath. Laurie shakes her head in embarrassment, casts a wistful glance over the snow globe and hands it to the pouting girl.

"All right, here you go. I just wanted to give it to you. It is really beautiful. Do you know what that is inside the glass?" Laurie gently taps the glass with her finger and looks at the silenced child.

"I don't care what it is. I just want to see it snow!" The obnoxious child tears the treasure out of Laurie's hand, turns around and snorts as she struts away. Out of thin air, a woman appears, who seems to be the little girl's mother. She takes the ball carelessly from the hands of her child and puts it in their shopping cart just as irreverently.

Laurie looks around ashamed, but notices that all the customers are busy again with their own bargain hunting. Only the old woman behind the counter seems to have noticed that anything has happened.

Wednesday

When Laurie comes out of the bathroom, she watches Bella as she admires her tooth again, for at least the hundredth time. She hears Bella's whisper to her father's picture, but she cannot make out the words. Laurie grants Bella a little privacy with her deceased father and goes quietly into the kitchen area.

From a drawer she takes a small box that she has kept for this purpose and heads back to the dining room. Leaning against the door frame, she clears her throat to announce her return. Bella looks up at her mother with those ever-sparkling eyes.

She gives Bella a loving smile, but notices the sadness in her dark eyes. The little girl bites her lower lip.

"What do you think of us giving your tooth to the Tooth Fairy today?" Laurie holds the box up and winks at her thoughtful daughter, who shrugs her small shoulders and mumbles, "Sure." Bella slowly gets up from the chair and brings the tooth to her mother.

"What's wrong, Bella?" Laurie crouches down to meet her daughter at eye level, gently stroking her curly hair and watching the curls bounce back.

"Anne told everyone at school today that the Tooth Fairy is a stupid cow because she gave her an ugly Barbie and not the one she actually wanted and that she purposely broke her and..." The little girl pulls her shoulders up again and is close to tears. "What if the Tooth Fairy heard that and now won't bring gifts to any kid? It's not nice to talk like that. I think I would have liked that Barbie." She draws air in noisily, then rubs the back of her hand under her nose. wiping away her sadness.

"No, saying that isn't nice. But you know, the Tooth Fairy gives every child exactly what she deserves, and not necessarily what she wants. Here." Laurie hands her little girl the box from the kitchen. "Let's put it outside the door. It's too windy on the window sill. It would be a tragedy if the wind blew it down." She winks at the kid. "And then tomorrow we'll see, if she's a cow or a fairy."

Thursday

The familiar sound of a door opening wakes Laurie up. She feels a cold breeze on her face. She keeps her eyes closed and waits for Bella's reaction. The joyful squeals of a happy child fill the room, bringing a smile to the mother's face. The door is closed again and the winter cold settles in the living room. Laurie waits for Bella's next action.

Bella tip-toes slowly to the pull-out couch and puts something heavy on the blanket covering her sleeping mother. Laurie frowns in surprise, but does not dare to move.

"Mom?" Bella gently strokes her mother's head and whispers softly in her ear, "Mom, she was here … and left me something very heavy. She took my tooth and left two letters. Mom, are you awake?"

Laurie has to concentrate to restrain her emotion. What had she forgotten at the door? Why are there two letters? Something is wrong here. What went wrong? She takes a deep breath and blinks sleepily at the enchanted face of her beloved girl. Sparkling eyes and a gaped-tooth smile are caught in her gaze.

"Oh, how wonderful. May I see?" Laurie begins to pull the blanket away when the little girl stops her.

"No, don't! Otherwise it will fall down! I put it here, on your legs. Look!" Her little fingers point to the blanket. Laurie leans up and actually sees two letters, but not the one she put down herself. Next to them is a box with a pink bow around it. She puts on a happy face and, feigning amazement, tries to contribute to the joy.

"Wow! I wonder what that means? Do you want me to read you the letters first? Oh look, one of them is for me." Although quite curious about the envelope addressed to her, Laurie reaches for the unfamiliar envelope with the inscription "BELLA" and waits for her daughter to nod before she opens it.

*Dear Bella, thank you for this great tooth! You have done very well and I am very proud of you.*

Laurie smiles at her daughter, who is almost bursting with happiness, and continues to read with astonishment and curiosity,

"I know you wished for a Barbie, but my fairy dust has decided to bring you this gift. I'm sure that your mom knows the magic in it and it will give you both much joy. I sincerely wish you an enchanting Christmas season and a lovely Christmas with your grandparents.

With love, your Tooth Fairy."

"We're going to Grandma and Grandpa's house?" Bella's squeals of joy fill the small apartment. Before Laurie can contradict her, the package is open and her girl's eyes are almost out of her head. "Mom! Look at this!" Laurie slowly lets the letter, still in her hand, sink into her lap, while her mouth falls open in amazement. She watches as Bella holds a glass ball in both hands and looks at it from all sides.

21

She turns the ball upside- down for a moment, then squeals with delight when she sees it snowing inside. "Look, Mom, it's snowing in the ball. It is snowing on this pointed tower! Look, how beautiful."

The surprised mother is speechless. Then Bella holds out the second envelope. "What did she write to you, Mom?"

Laurie blinks back some rising tears. She opens the envelope with her name on it. When she sees what's inside, her trembling hand slowly covers her mouth.

"Mommy? Why are you crying? Is it not good? What's in there?" Bella gently clings to her mother with one hand and holds the beautiful snowball securely with the other.

Laurie draws a short but noisy breath through her nose and wipes away her tears. "It's great, sweetie! You have the best Tooth Fairy of all time, you know that." She lays two airline tickets carefully on the side table, then lays her hand over Bella's, both now holding the magic ball.

"Sweetie, your Tooth Fairy wrote, 'I would know the magic in this ball.'" Laurie taps her index finger on the glass. "This pointed tower is called the Eiffel Tower. It's in Paris, which is a beautiful city in Europe. It was under this tower I told your Dad that you were going to be born." At these words, tears fill her eyes again, which Bella does not see, because her big saucer eyes are fixed on the snow globe. Bella can see the magic now.

"Ohhh, under this Eiffel Tower, we were all together ..."

Friday

"Holy sh--! That's not possible! You're kidding me, right? No, who could that have been?  Who knew everything about the tooth and the snow globe and where your parents live and... I mean, I would just love to be your hero in this story, but it wasn't me.  And I've never seen this snow globe before.  Sorry.  I have to buy Christmas presents at the House of Hope myself this year.  I hope they have decent boxes, too..."

"Mary.  Seriously!  What should I do now?  Do you think I should go to the police?  I mean, someone could be messing with me." Laurie rubs both hands over her face and then tucks her hair behind her ears.  Biting her lower lip, she looks desperately out the diner window at the busy street, searching for answers.

"What now?  You aren't seriously not going?  Hey, smart one, these tickets are in your name and you can't disappoint your baby.  I may be old, but I'm young enough to believe in a Christmas miracle.  And this is a miracle.  A darn good one.

Maybe a little crazy, but you should accept it gratefully. If your Tooth Fairy wants to reveal herself, she or he will do that sooner or later. If not, then you can still go to the police. But right now, you should put on a pretty face and go home. Your suitcases won't pack themselves."

Mary quickly waves to the waitress that the check is paid, then turns back to Laurie and points her finger outside.

"Look at them, those people! Christmas stress! Who actually invented it? I wish I could just enjoy a contemplative, carefree, childlike Christmas again. Instead. I have to get back to work, so there will be food on our table, let alone presents under the tree. Send me a picture, when you are happily drinking eggnog around the Christmas tree." She rises, wraps her scarf several times around her neck, pulls her cap on and slips into a worn coat. Bending down to kiss her friend on the cheek, Mary whispers, "You get what you deserve. Love you!"

"Love you, too. Thanks Mary, and Merry Christmas." Laurie waves to Mary as she leaves, then stands to put her coat on as well. The young server walks up to clear the table, then looks sheepishly at Laurie.

"I'm very sorry, but your friend didn't leave enough money for the bill. She probably just confused the one with a ten." The waitress lays the bill and single dollar bill in front of Laurie on the table.

"Oh, I am very sorry. Wait, I'll give you the rest. Yeah, she was in a hurry and probably didn't notice." Laurie digs some coins out of her coat pocket and reaches for her purse to look for the rest. "Here. Keep the change. I'm sorry it isn't more. Merry Christmas."

As Laurie steps out of the diner into the street, the cold air hits her face.

She thinks about how best to get to the airport. Maybe Roger, the apartment manager, would drive her if she promises him delicious cookies from grandma?

Saturday

As soon as the doorbell rang, the excited Bella races out of her room, pulling a small, pink suitcase and calling to her mother.

"Mom, hurry up! He's here! Come on, or we'll miss the plane!" Bella opens the door hastily and beams at the old man in front of her.

"I got a call from Santa Claus. He asked me to drive two angels to the airport. Do you have any idea who he meant by that? Santa did say, one of them has a big gap in her mouth!" The old man opens his mouth and presents his own missing tooth and otherwise partly silver teeth to the squealing Bella.

"That's me! And mommy! We're the angels. But I am the one with the tooth gap. Can you see? Right here." The little girl points to her missing tooth and looks back into the apartment. Before she can shout again to her mother, Laurie steps out of the bathroom.

"I'm coming. I'm coming. Good morning Roger. Thanks for taking the time to drive us. You're the angel." She takes her hat and coat off the hook by the door and grabs her waiting bag. Casting a final glance into the small apartment, her eyes linger a moment on the framed photograph on the table.

***

"Your Tooth Fairy gave you and your mom this flight? I sure would have liked to have a Tooth Fairy like that. Mine just put a dollar under my pillow for me."

28

Laughing politely, the pretty flight attendant puts an apple juice in front of Bella and winks at Laurie.

Laurie smiles back, a little embarrassed, and says mostly to Bella, "The plane tickets were actually for me, weren't they, Sweetie?" Then she wonders how she will ever be able to explain any future presents from the Tooth Fairy. She looks out through the airplane window and tries to rejoice over this great gift. But thoughts of joy are based off by vague apprehension.

"Mommy, aren't you glad that I have such a great Tooth Fairy?" The overjoyed girl says looking at her mother for a moment before turning back to Tom & Jerry on the small screen in front of her.

Laurie closes her eyes and tries to remember how she felt when she learned that there was no Tooth Fairy or Santa Claus or even Rudolph. Not to mention that you don't really hear the ocean in a seashell when you press it to your ear.

Sunday

Bella and Grandpa's happy voices echo throughout the house as Laurie sleepily pulls back her blanket. She slept surprisingly well, although after all these years she found it strange to be in her childhood bedroom again. When she visited with Adam and Bella, in the years before, the three of them stayed in the converted basement. But for her and Bella, her old bed was wonderful.

"I miss you, Ady ... How am I going to do all this without you here?" She flinches as she senses movement behind her.

Her mother is standing in the open door looking sympathetically at her. "And we miss you too. What's keeping you in that big city now? We have enough space here, and we can help take care of Bella. You'll be able to find a job again. There are also wonderful bookstores here. I'm sure someone is looking for an expert like you."

Laurie puts on her robe and slips into the cuddly slippers next to the bed. "Let's go downstairs, Ma. Otherwise those two will open our presents." Laurie heads toward the door, but her mother stands frozen.

"Laurie, where did you get the plane tickets from? I want you to be honest with me. I won't tell your father, but please, don't give me another Tooth Fairy lie. What have you done?"

"Nothing, Ma! I'm just as baffled as you are. I don't know where they came from. For real! But how can you believe, that I did something indecent?" Laurie looks aghast at her mother's pale face, and squeezes passed her, rolling her eyes. "Really, Ma!"

"I know. I know, dear. I'm sorry. But I can't make sense of it. Who would just give you two plane tickets? It's 2019! No one just gives someone something without expecting anything in return." She shakes her head vigorously and shrugs her shoulders, "Nobody's that generous. Even if it is Christmas."

"I know, Ma. I know. But let's just try to enjoy the next few days for Bella. And when I'm back in the city, I'll try to sort it all out. Promise!" Now her mother allows Laurie to lead her down the stairs. Together they face the merry chatter in the cozy living room.

Just before they reach the last stair, she hears her mother whispering behind her, "You remember when you packed your bags and wanted to live in the tree house forever, because you caught

Dad trying to replace your tooth with roller skates..."

Monday

After a long walk, the four family members sit down at the kitchen table and enjoy some hot chocolate with lots of tiny marshmallows in it.  Laurie's Dad gets up and takes a tall bottle of clear liquid from the wooden buffet against the wall.

"Well,    it's    still    Christmas somewhere, isn't it?"   He winks at his giggling granddaughter and pours a good sip for himself into a separate glass.

"Grandma?  Laurie?" He holds up the bottle, offering in the direction of the two women.  His wife shakes her head and raises her hand slightly in a polite pass.  His daughter nods in acceptance.

"Why not. My nerves could stand to settle down a little before I sit down to do all that paperwork. Thanks Dad." She takes the glass.

"What's paperwork Mommy?" Bella loudly sips her chocolate and squints out from behind a big 'Frosty the Snowman' mug.

"I've got a lot of questions that I have to answer, so that the nice woman from the employment agency can help me to find a new job. And because it's a lot of paper, I call it paperwork." Laurie empties her nerve drink in one gulp. Then notices the questioning look on her mother's face.

"I'm thinking about it, Ma. Promise. But I have to fill it out one way or another, otherwise I won't get any unemployment benefits." Turning to her father and Bella, she asks, "And what adventures do you two have planned for today? I saw you whispering while we were all walking." Raising her eyebrow, she lets her index finger swing between Bella and her grandfather. Bella chuckles into her soon-to-be-empty mug and shrugs mischievously.

***

"Well then, let's do this!" Laurie is sitting on the comfy sofa in front of the blazing fire in her Christmas leggings, a Rudolph sweater, and her new knit socks. Talking to herself, she begins answering the employment agency's questions. "Personality is already filled out, that's helpful...Marital status: widowed...Single parent...Profession: Book expert...desired schedule: flexible, as long as possible to complement school hours...Travel availability: no car... Geez...I wouldn't hire me... hopefully someone has a little heart...Wait a minute...but...where do I know?...I have seen that before..." Thinking aloud, Laurie holds up the preprinted questionnaire in the air and to the light from the window.

Fine, delicate lines can be seen along the lower edge of the paper. A justice scale as a watermark, with the slogan, "Blessed & Justice" and as a symbol, in bold letters "B&J".

Frowning, she puts the paperwork aside and slips out from under the warm blanket. She walks out of the living room into the hallway and reaches into her purse. She takes the envelope out, in which the two airline tickets from the Tooth Fairy were. She opens her mouth in amazement. As she puts two and two together, she begins to shake her head, marveling at the realization. Interrupting her thoughts, her mobile phone rings in the living room. Mary's number shows up, so she takes the call.

Tuesday

At the airport, Bella, Laurie, and her parents exchange goodbye hugs and kisses. Laurie's father puts an envelope into her coat pocket and winks at her. "But don't tell your Ma about it. Otherwise she'll be upset because you wouldn't take it from her. Come home soon, Angel, it was very nice to have you with us." He puts his arm around his wife as she sheds a tear of farewell and pulls her close. "Come on, it's not that bad being alone with me." Laurie's mother lets out a grunt between tears and waves goodbye to her daughter and granddaughter.

***

"Bella, dear, could you imagine living with Grandma and Grandpa? With me too, of course!" Laurie tries to give her question a casualness while buttering the small roll from her in-flight meal. When she gets no reaction, she looks at her daughter in the seat next to her. Bella's wide-eyed eyes stare at her mother in amazement, her curly-haired head nods eagerly and her bread-stuffed mouth threatens to burst. Laurie laughs heartily at this sight, yet at the same time suppressing her rising tears. "I'm guessing that's YES? Or no? Or maybe?" She's still grinning, tilting her head slightly as if making a difficult decision.

In the meantime, Bella has choked down her bite of bread and now squeaks happily, "YES, YES, YES!"

"I am glad to hear that. I would like that too and I know who else would be happy about it too."

"Grandma and Grandpa!" Her daughter replied beaming and cuddling her new plush panther.

"But first we have to visit someone when we're back in the city. Because you know, Sweetie, these airline tickets weren't from your Tooth Fairy. My name was on the envelope, but I didn't give her a tooth, right? It was a coincidence that everything came at the same time. Your snow globe and my envelope." She strokes her surprised daughter's rosy cheeks. "There is a particularly nice man at the employment agency. He gave us this trip and we should personally thank him for that."

Bella nods satisfied and smiles, "There are so many angels in this world, huh, Mommy?"


Wednesday

With a nervously pounding heart and dry throat, Laurie opens the door to the employment agency, "Blessed & Justice" and lets her daughter take the lead. At the reception desk, they are greeted warmly by an elderly, plump woman who looks through her thick glasses at Bella and asks in wonderment, "Well, aren't you a little too young to need a job, Miss?" She rises from her chair and hands a lollipop to the giggling curly-haired girl. She smiles at Laurie and points with her pen to the glass door on the other side of the corridor. "Go ahead, Dear. He's waiting for you."

Laurie gently knocks on the frosted glass door and sees a shadow moving behind it. Shortly thereafter, the door opens and a familiar face shines with joyful greeting, "Welcome, ladies. Please come in. Have a seat. I was hoping the two of you would be coming to visit me. How was your Christmas? How was the flight?" His excited chattering tells Laurie that he too is very nervous, which calms her down.

"We had a wonderful Christmas, Sir! Thanks to you, we even had a marvelous Christmas. We could have only dreamed of going home." Laurie sits down on her assigned chair and shows Bella the chair next to her. "Sir, I don't know how I should ... well, what to say ... how I can ever thank you for that. It will be a long time before I can pay you back..." Before she can finish her sentence, she is interrupted by the man behind the table with his raised hand.

"I am very pleased to hear that you and your family had a beautiful, wonderful Christmas. That was my goal and I love reaching goals, you know?" He smirks mischievously and Laurie tries to remember where she has seen this face before.

"We have a Christmas program in which our employees can make a proposal. This means that all our personnel consultants can make a suggestion from their customer files who they feel could use a Christmas miracle. It was not difficult for us this year. We decided that it was clearly you two ladies who deserved a little Christmas magic." He spreads his arms, gesturing to the two opposite him.

At that moment, there is a knock on the door and Laurie's personal agent enters. With tears in her eyes, Laurie gets up and hugs her wordlessly. Likewise, without words, her embrace is returned.

Leaving the office, Laurie's agent takes Bella by the hand and walks with her toward the exit. The leader of "Blessed & Justice" holds Laurie back by the arm and places a small box into her hand. Surprised, she looks at it and recognizes the box immediately. "But ...where..." She quickly puts the box in her coat pocket and makes sure that her daughter didn't notice.

"I must confess, I overheard you in the street when you left our office last week. I was on my way to a meeting, right behind you, listening to your conversation with your mother. And, that you said you would go to the House of Hope. The woman there remembered you very well and also the little monster who nearly got the snow globe. The mother ended up deciding at the register not to buy it, but you had already left the shop. I bought it later that day."

He grinned at Laurie and said goodbye with the words,

"You get, what you deserve!"

\*\*\*

\*\*\*

# Merry Christmas!

\*\*\*

Hiam Mondini is a Swiss author and is living temporarily in Chicago.

She started a Christmas story series inspired by scenes observed in everyday life or experienced herself. Her second Christmas in Chicagoland is just around the corner, and she is trying to keep a watchful eye on the happenings around her, as well as finding inspiration to spread joy to others.


Emily Ulbert is an American writer, living in Chicagoland.

She loves Christmas and the magic that surrounds it. She jumped at the opportunity to contribute to the English version of this story. She tries, each, Christmas, to create and spread the spirit of the season and all year long. And stories, like this one, serve as a reminder to not just live in your own world.

Chicago – N Michigan Ave 2019

Drawing by

Aurelio Romano Mondini, 92 Yrs